ALIEN NEXT DOOR

THE MARVELOUS MUSEUM

by A. I. Newton

illustrated by Alan Brown

little bee books

TABLE OF CONTENTS

1
THE JOURNEY HOME

A GLEAMING SPACESHIP sped through space. It had just blasted off from the planet Tragas. Its destination: Earth.

On board the ship were Harris Walker and his best friend Roxy Martinez. They were from Earth and were now on their way home. Also on board were their friend Zeke and his parents. They were aliens from Tragas.

"I still can't believe that even though we've been gone for weeks, it will only feel like a short time to our parents back on Earth," said Roxy.

"Yes," said Zeke. "Time moves differently in space. And my dad discovered a wormhole that will get you home, with only a half hour having passed on Earth since you left."

Zeke's parents were researchers who moved from planet to planet studying different kinds of aliens. They had come to Earth to research human culture. Zeke met Harris and Roxy when he joined their second-grade class at Jefferson Elementary School.

When Zeke had first moved next door to Harris, Harris was suspicious that this new kid might be an alien. In fact, he did everything he could to prove it. But when he finally found out that Zeke *really was* an alien, Harris began doing all he could to protect Zeke's secret—even from his best friend Roxy! Roxy only found out the truth about Zeke just before they all blasted off from Earth for Tragas.

When it was time for Zeke and his parents to leave Earth, Harris and Roxy snuck on board their spaceship and ended up traveling to Tragas, where they saw Zeke's home planet.

The three friends now streaked through space. Nobody really wanted to think about the fact that when they reached Earth, Harris and Roxy would be home. But Zeke would be blasting off again, heading to the next planet his parents were assigned to research.

"I'm happy that we don't have to hide anymore," said Harris. "Now that your parents know we are on board. I want to check out the ship!"

"Sure," said Zeke.

Zeke, who had taken a human form while on Earth, was now in his natural Tragonian form. He had green skin and six tentacles. He had five eyes and his ears were two antennae. He had no legs. He hovered above the ground.

Zeke led his friends to the ship's 4-D holo-projection movie theater.

"With this projector, you feel like you are right in the middle of the movie!" said Zeke.

"Like the one you had in your room on Earth!" said Roxy.

"Exactly," said Zeke.

"I remember," said Harris. "We watched a holo-movie called *Danger in the Deep!*"

"I felt like I was underwater, surrounded by sea monsters!" said Roxy.

"Well, get ready for another adventure!" Zeke said.

He pressed a button, and the three friends suddenly found themselves in a dense jungle. Strange, flying creatures swooped right past their heads.

"This one is called Valley of the Flying Cratega Beasts," said Zeke.

"Wow! It feels so real!" said Roxy, ducking to get out of the way of a giant wing.

After the movie, Zeke then showed his friends the ship's interstellar schoolroom. This was where the history of Tragas could be quickly absorbed in meditation pods. It was used to keep up children's education on long space trips.

"This sure looks a lot easier than going to school!" said Harris.

Mentioning school reminded him that the next time he went to class, Zeke wouldn't be there. In fact, he wouldn't even be on planet Earth! Harris started to feel sad.

"I'm really going to miss you, buddy," Harris said to Zeke.

"Me too," replied Zeke.

"I have an idea to try to perk us up," said Roxy, who was also feeling sad.

"Let's play a game. How about hide-and-seek?"

"Yeah!" said Harris.

"Hide-and-seek?" asked Zeke.

"It's an Earth game where people hide, and one person tries to find them all," Roxy explained. "I'll be 'it' first."

"'It'?" asked Zeke.

"'It' is the person who does the looking," said Roxy. "Now you and Harris go hide, somewhere you think I won't look. I'll count to one hundred and then try to find you."

Harris and Zeke ran off, and Roxy started counting.

"Now, where would someone hide on an alien spaceship?" Roxy asked herself when she reached one hundred. She set off to find her friends.

2 HIDE . . . AND ZEKE

"THE GOAL OF THIS GAME
is to prevent Roxy from finding me,"
Zeke said to himself as he raced around
the ship. "I know just the place."

He came to a chamber that said Miniaturization above it and climbed in. The chamber was normally used to shrink bulky cargo for storage on long journeys through space. But Zeke had other plans. He pressed a button and shrunk himself! When the process was done, he was just two inches tall. He stepped from the chamber and started to move around the spaceship.

"I usually know where I'm going on this ship," he said. "But being this tiny, everything looks different."

Zeke came to his parents' office. It was empty. His parents were on the ship's bridge guiding its flight through space.

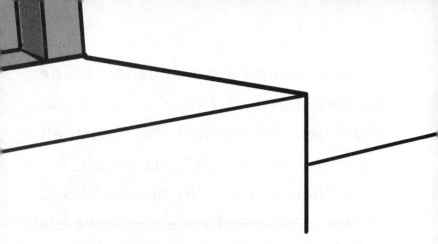

A small step at the base of the door became his first obstacle. At his normal size, Zeke would easily float right over the step. But now, he had to use all his strength to float up to the top of the step. Exhausted, he tumbled down the other side and landed on the office floor.

"That was tough," he said to himself. "Now to find a good place to hide." He looked up and saw a very high shelf. "There! That's it."

Zeke climbed up a panel, using its switches and knobs as hand and footholds. He reached the high shelf and sat down to catch his breath.

Suddenly, a display screen blazed to life, projected in the air above his head.

"I must have hit the On button when I climbed," he said.

A message labeled IMPORTANT flashed on the screen in Tragonian. Zeke read the message.

"Wow!" he said in a tiny voice. "This sounds really cool!"

Meanwhile, Harris wandered through the unfamiliar spaceship looking for a place to hide. He found an empty storage room and stepped in.

When he heard Roxy's footsteps coming down a passageway, he closed the door and pressed his back against the far wall. A bright yellow light began flashing.

Uh-oh! Harris thought. *What did I just do?*

Turning around, he saw a button labeled *Gravity Control*. The yellow light stopped flashing, and Harris floated up to the chamber's ceiling.

Wow! he thought, looking down. *I must have turned off the gravity in this room. And since we're in space . . . there is no gravity! So even if she comes into this room, Roxy won't think to look for me up here. This is a great hiding spot. The only question is—how will I get down?!*

Roxy wandered from passageway to passageway, peeking into dark rooms, storage bins, and overhead compartments. She checked every nook and cranny she came across.

Then Roxy approached the half-open door to Zeke's parents' office and noticed a glow coming from within.

Hmm… she thought. *Maybe someone is hiding in there!*

3 AN INVITATION

OPENING THE DOOR SLOWLY, Roxy quietly stepped into the office. There, floating in midair, was the projection screen Zeke had opened. On the screen was a blinking message. Roxy grabbed a pair of translation glasses and read it:

Xad and Quar,
You are invited to the opening of our brand-new exhibit PLANET EARTH. Since it is based on your research, we would be honored if you could attend.

It will take place on
Galactic Date: 344-119-773.9

Sincerely,
Thaddrix, Director, Museum of Galactic Culture, Kretlak Prime

"Wow, a whole alien exhibit about Earth! This would be so cool to see," Roxy said to herself.

"It sure would," said a squeaky voice from behind and above her. Zeke, still new to hide-and-seek, couldn't control his excitement.

"That kind of sounded like Zeke," Roxy said to herself.

She spun around but couldn't find where he was hiding in the room. "Zeke?" she asked, confused. "I guess I found you. But I don't see you."

Then she looked up and spotted tiny Zeke sitting on a high shelf.

"Okay, first, I *did* find you," said Roxy. "And second, what in the world happened to you?"

Zeke explained about how he used the ship's miniaturization chamber.

"I thought it would be a good way to hide," he said. "And it was, except for the whole talking-when-you-came-in-the-room thing."

"Well, now that I found you," said Roxy. "What about that message? Wouldn't it be cool to see all your parents' research on display?"

"That would be so great for them," replied Zeke. "We have to find Harris and tell him, then go talk to my parents."

Roxy stuck out her hand. Zeke jumped down into her palm.

"It'll be faster if we travel this way," she said, slipping Zeke into her shirt pocket. His tiny head peeked over the top of the pocket. "Come on, let's go find Harris."

They searched the ship and soon came to the storage room where Harris was hiding. Roxy pulled the door open and peeked into the room. She didn't see Harris. Just to make sure, she stepped into the room and immediately floated up, where she joined Harris on the ceiling.

"I found you, Harris," Roxy said. "But why are we on the ceiling?!"

"I leaned against that wall," Harris explained, pointing. "I must have hit that button."

"That button turns off the gravity in the room," Zeke explained in his high, squeaky voice.

Harris saw tiny Zeke peeking out of Roxy's pocket.

"What happened to you?" he asked in shock.

"I'll explain later," squeaked Zeke. "Right now, I've got to get the gravity back on in this room."

Zeke scrambled out of Roxy's pocket, then climbed across the wall and down, using the handles on the storage bins. He reached the Gravity Control button and pressed it.

They all floated slowly down to the floor.

"Come on," said Zeke, as Roxy slipped him back into her pocket. "Let's go talk to my parents!"

As the three friends hurried toward the ship's bridge, Roxy filled Harris in on Zeke's shrinking and the museum's invitation.

"Seeing the exhibit based on all the research they did on Earth would kind of be the icing on the cake for your parents," Harris said.

Zeke was confused. "I know what cake is," he said. "And I know what icing looks like on cake, but what does that have to do with my parents' research?"

Harris and Roxy smiled. "Just another Earth expression," said Harris.

4 COURSE CORRECTION

HARRIS, ROXY, AND ZEKE

quickly made their way to the ship's bridge. There they found Xad and Quar at the controls. Zeke's parents were also in their natural Tragonian forms.

"Zekelabraxis!" exclaimed Xad, using Zeke's full Tragonian name. He was confused at the sight of his son small enough to fit into Roxy's pocket. "What is the meaning of this?"

Zeke laughed. He had gotten so excited about the museum, he forgot that he had shrunk himself to play hide-and-seek. He quickly explained what happened during the game, and then told his parents about the invitation to the museum.

"It would be so exciting to see all your hard work on display at the Museum of Galactic Culture. Like icing on a cake," Zeke said, looking at Harris and Roxy.

"Icing … cake?" Quar asked, confused. She thought hard. "We did cover Earth desserts in our research, but there are many other things at the exhibit we are looking forward to seeing."

"It's just an Earth expression," Zeke explained, still not completely sure himself what it meant. "So, when were you planning on going to Kretlak Prime to see the exhibit?"

"We don't know," said Xad. "We must get Harris and Roxy back to Earth as soon as we can."

"Where is Kretlak Prime anyway?" asked Roxy.

Quar put her tentacles up to her head and mind-projected a star field.

"There," she said, pointing at a planet with red oceans and orange landmasses.

Xad and Quar studied the star field carefully.

"I think we should go see the exhibit," said Zeke.

"It would be cool to see what everyone thinks of Earth customs and culture," added Harris.

"We take all that stuff for granted, having grown up on Earth," said Roxy. "But I'd love to see what people from other planets think of Earth."

"People from all over the galaxy do go to Kretlak Prime to visit the museum," Quar explained.

"Well, this is interesting," said Xad, pointing at the image of Kretlak Prime.

The planet hung in space, right next to a wormhole.

"Kretlak Prime is just outside the entrance to the wormhole we will be using to get Harris and Roxy back home. So we could stop there, then take the wormhole and still get you home with very little time having passed on Earth."

"And we'd all get to spend more time together before we have to say goodbye," Zeke said to his two friends.

"Yay!" all three kids shouted.

"Then it's agreed," said Quar. "We are going to the Museum of Galactic Culture!"

"Yes," said Xad. "But just one more thing."

"What is it?" squeaked Zeke.

"Zekelabraxis, please go return to your normal size!"

5 THE MUSEUM OF GALACTIC CULTURE

FOLLOWING ANOTHER WEEK of space travel, with many games and movies to pass the time, they finally approached Kretlak Prime. As they dropped into the planet's atmosphere, the three friends stared out the ship's front viewscreen. Vibrant white oceans and jagged purple landmasses filled their field of vision. The planet grew bigger and bigger as the ship descended.

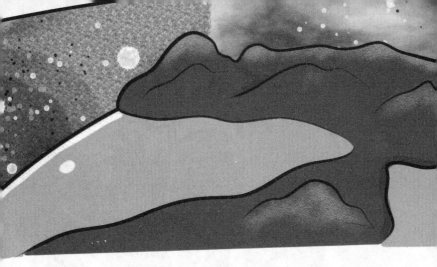

"I've never seen a white-and-purple planet," said Harris.

"Well, you actually haven't seen that many planets at all," Roxy pointed out.

"Well, I have seen a bunch of planets," said Zeke, now back to his normal size. "But I've never seen one that looks like this."

Xad and Quar guided the ship down to the surface. A huge complex soon came into view.

"There's the museum!" cried Zeke, pointing at a sprawling building.

They landed in a large spaceport connected to the museum. Hundreds of spaceships of all different types, from many planets, filled the parking area. Leaving their ship, Zeke and the others approached the entrance to the museum.

A sprawling 3-D holo-projected replica of the galaxy spread out to welcome them. Planets spun in orbit in a glittering star field.

"Wow!" said Roxy. "If this is just the entrance, I can't wait to see what's actually inside!"

They passed through a shimmering curtain of golden light and entered the museum. Above their heads, huge silver rings spun and rotated, releasing energy waves that radiated out in all directions.

"What are those?" Harris asked, looking up.

"They are translo-rings," Xad explained. "They act as a universal translation system. Visitors from all planets can understand each other, no matter what language they speak."

The group was greeted by an alien with a tall, green, stalklike body and many wiggling fingers extending from the body.

"Welcome to the museum," the alien said. "Let's get you all fitted with hover-boots."

Wow! thought Harris. *Those translo-rings really work. I'm sure this guy is not speaking English.*

Everyone was given hover-boots based on their shoe sizes. The hover-boots slipped over their regular shoes. They allowed visitors to zoom around the enormous museum quickly, floating a few inches above the ground.

Zeke and his parents also slipped on hover-boots. Although they could float, the boots allowed them to concentrate on the exhibits, rather than on floating for such a long period of time.

The group hovered over to a huge directory—a miniature model of the museum itself—showing the location of all the exhibits.

"I see exhibits about a few of the planets you have lived on, Zeke," said Roxy. "I'd like to see those."

"Look, Xad, Quar!" shouted Zeke, pointing to a section of the directory. "There is your new exhibit on Earth!"

A bright, flashing *JUST OPENED* sign blinked above the replica of the Earth exhibit.

"It is exciting," said Quar. "But I think we should save that for last. What would you kids like to see first?"

"I'd actually love to see the exhibit on Tragas," said Harris. "We only got to spend a little bit of time there."

"Of course," said Quar.

The group headed to the Tragas exhibit, speeding along in their hover-boots. As they traveled through the museum, they passed aliens from all over the galaxy. This was nothing unusual for Zeke. He had already lived on a number of planets and seen aliens of all types. But for Roxy and Harris, it was an amazing experience.

They saw a family of aliens who appeared to be nothing more than glowing energy blobs. They floated together like shiny clouds. When this family arrived at an exhibit, eyeballs suddenly popped out of their blob-like forms so they could see the exhibits better.

Another alien passed them, looking like a walking tree trunk. It towered over almost all the other visitors. When it came to a low archway, it shrunk in height. Then it grew back to its normal height on the other side of the archway.

They saw a family of fishlike aliens who appeared to be swimming through the air. They wore fishbowl helmets filled with water on their heads so they could breathe outside of their normal, watery environment.

"Wow!" said Harris. "The visitors are just as educational as the exhibits!"

6 MUSEUM TOUR

ZEKE, HIS PARENTS, AND his friends arrived at the Tragas exhibit. Zeke smiled seeing how the culture of his planet was represented.

"This is great!" said Roxy. "It's like being able to visit the whole planet again in a short amount of time."

Many of the things that Roxy and Harris had seen on Tragas were represented in the exhibit: yellow waterfalls flowing up instead of down; giant mice as big as dogs; a replica of a stadium where Bonkas—the most popular game on Tragas—was played; and holographic images of Tragaslovox, the founder of Tragas, giving a lecture.

They turned a corner and stopped in their tracks.

"Wow! Look at that!" said Harris. "I know what *that* is!"

There, bellowing a terrifying roar, was a life-sized replica of a Kraka Beast. Harris had been fascinated by this Tragonian monster ever since Zeke told the story of the beast around a campfire on their Beaver Scouts camping trip.

The giant, fifteen-foot-tall replica moved and snarled like the real thing. It munched on a striped pritchik tree, which it held in one hand, and then took a bite out of a flying car, which it held in the other.

A huge crowd gathered around the Kraka Beast exhibit.

"I'd hate to run into that guy on a dark night," said Harris, shivering, but laughing at the same time.

Soon they finished the Tragas exhibit.

"I'd like to see the exhibit on Charbock," said Roxy, as she hovered along. "From Zeke's description it sounds pretty cool."

"That's the planet where you lived right before you came to Earth, right?" asked Harris. He recalled the conversation he and Zeke had had when Zeke had finally admitted he really was from another planet.

"That's right," said Zeke. "I met some nice kids there, but none of them became such good friends, like you and Roxy."

The Charbock exhibit featured teleportation technology that Zeke had told Harris about.

Roxy stepped into a metal booth. A curved door slid closed around her, followed by a blinding flash of light. When the door slid open again, Roxy found that she was no longer in the same booth. She had been teleported into an identical booth on the other side of the Charbock exhibit.

"Wow!" said Roxy, stepping from the second booth. "I bet they don't have any traffic jams on Charbock if people can get around this way!"

"Yeah, and no one is ever late for school!" added Harris, stepping into the booth to take his turn.

They moved on to the next section of the Charbock exhibit. This part was Harris's favorite. Stepping into an enclosed area, he slipped a helmet onto his head.

"On Charbock, people can control the weather with their minds," Zeke explained. "It looks like that helmet allows museum visitors to do the same."

Harris imagined a bright, sunny day. Suddenly, a brilliant glow filled the whole area.

"I didn't think I'd need to bring sunscreen to a museum," said Roxy, shading her eyes with her hands.

Harris next thought about a blizzard he was once caught in on the way home from school. Snow started falling in thick flakes, piling up on the ground. Everyone had to float higher and higher to avoid having their hover-boots buried in snow!

Harris took off the helmet and they all stepped from the enclosed area, shaking the snow off their clothing. Confused visitors peered at the white stuff piling up, trying to figure out what had just happened.

"That would really come in handy back on Earth," said Harris, brushing off the last bits of snow.

"I know you," said Roxy. "You'd make every day a snow day and we'd never go to school!"

"Yeah," said Harris, smiling at the thought.

The group hovered along, looking at the exhibits of a few other planets. Then it was time to visit Xad and Quar's Earth exhibit.

7 EARTHLY WONDERS

XAD AND QUAR GREW MORE nervous the closer they got to the Earth exhibit. But Zeke was getting more and more excited. He really was proud of the work his parents did, even though it did mean that he had to move from planet to planet a lot.

They entered the exhibit by floating under a giant, spinning replica of planet Earth.

"Wow!" said Harris, looking up at the blue oceans and familiar continents. "It kind of makes me homesick."

The exhibit began in a long hallway. There, they saw replicas of a series of storefronts. Above them, holo-projected in the air, was a sign that began:

THE MALL:
WHERE EARTH PEOPLE GATHER

Roxy read the rest of the sign aloud:

"'A group of item acquisition establishments, which Earth people call "stores," where items of various kinds can be exchanged for small bits of green paper or even smaller plastic cards, is known on Earth as "the mall." We thought a walk through an Earth mall would be a good way to introduce you to various aspects of their culture.'"

"Let's start in here," said Zeke, pointing to a virtual doorway.

They all stepped through the doorway and found themselves immersed in a very realistic, 3-D holo-projected replica of a clothing store in a mall on Earth. A sign hovered in the air above them that read: *GARMENT SELECTION STORE*.

Harris read the sign aloud:

"'For some reason, which we were not able to understand, Earth people, also known as humans, feel a strong need to acquire clothing items of different shapes, sizes, and colors. Tragonians, of course, wear the same style and color clothes at all times.'"

Harris reached out and touched a rack filled with shirts. Instantly, a viewscreen appeared above his head showing shirts of many styles. He touched one of the images and the shirt suddenly appeared on him, replacing the shirt he was wearing.

A second screen then appeared, showing a rainbow of colors. "*Select color*," said a robotic voice. Each time Harris touched a color on the screen, his shirt changed to that color.

"Wow!" said Harris. "I wish it was really this easy to shop for clothing on Earth."

The group stepped back out into the hallway, then walked through the next doorway.

A holo-projected sign in the air above them read:

"Shouldn't that be 'sporting goods store'?" Roxy whispered to Harris.

Harris shrugged. "Yeah, but I guess it doesn't really matter."

Roxy picked up a baseball bat. A sign appeared above her head:

BASE BALL. An Earth game based on the ancient Tragonian game of Bonkas. In this simplified version, for reasons no one on Earth seems to know, the game is played with only one ball, as opposed to the traditional ten.

In an instant, they were all holographically projected into a baseball stadium. They were on the field, standing in front of a cheering crowd.

Roxy stood at home plate. A human-looking holographic pitcher threw a pitch, and Roxy smacked it for a home run. She put down the bat and the holograph changed, returning them to the sporting goods store.

Zeke picked up a tennis racket. "Wouldn't it be easier to hit a baseball with the big end of this stick?" he asked, never having had the chance to see a tennis match while on Earth.

Before anyone could answer, they were all transported to the stands of a packed tennis stadium. They watched two players smack the ball back and forth over the net.

"I still don't understand Earth sports," said Xad. "This sport uses only one ball but two sticks."

Zeke put down the racket, and the tennis stadium vanished.

Returning to the hallway, they came to a blinking sign that said: *NECESSARY NOURISHMENT*.

"Didn't you tell your folks that the place Earth people go to eat is called a 'restaurant'?" Harris asked Zeke.

"I did," Zeke replied. "But I guess something got lost in the translation."

"Let's eat!" said Roxy.

They all stepped into the "Necessary Nourishment" exhibit.

8
FOOD AND HISTORY

THE GROUP ENTERED WHAT looked like a school cafeteria.

"Zeke was a big help in preparing this part of the exhibit," explained Xad.

"I can see that," Harris whispered to Roxy. "This looks just like the cafeteria at Jefferson Elementary School."

"It feels like forever since we were last at school," Roxy said.

Moving along the line of food, they passed giant pretzels smothered in cheese and mustard.

"We had these at the Newtown Knights baseball game," Zeke said.

They saw hot dogs and marshmallows on sticks.

"And this was what we ate on the Beaver Scouts campout."

They came to a huge bagful of candy. "These I know from trick or treating."

A display of cheese and crackers was next.

"My parents served these the night your parents came to my house for dinner," Harris said to Zeke. Then he shook his head at the memory. "That was the night I accused you of being an alien in front of everyone."

Zeke smiled. "That sure feels like a long time ago," he said.

They next came to a stack of giant chocolate bars.

"And our school sold *these* to raise money for new band uniforms around Valentine's Day," said Roxy.

"Um, didn't you go out to an actual Earth restaurant in all the time you were there?" Roxy asked Zeke's parents.

"No need," said Quar. "We got all the research we needed from Zeke's experiences on Earth. Many thanks to you two, as well!"

They arrived at the end of the Earth culture portion of the exhibit. Rounding a bend, they came to the entrance to the final part of the exhibit. There, a big sign read:

PREVIOUS EARTH VISITS

"One of our favorite parts of learning about Earth's culture was discovering all the times people from other worlds have visited Earth in the past," Xad said to Harris and Roxy.

The two looked at each other, puzzled.

"For example, thousands of years ago the Jargons from the planet Jarcovia visited Earth and built this elliptical-shaped structure," Quar said. She pointed at a replica of the Colosseum being busily constructed by many aliens, who looked like walking bulls.

Quar continued. "And there were once giant sculptures of the Raplix people from the planet Plixamix made from ice. They are kind of a self-centered culture, so they always leave huge images of themselves on every planet they visit. But apparently they were unaware that ice melts!"

"The Pleadons from the planet Pleadurin left a message saying how much they enjoyed visiting Earth a long, long time ago," Xad added. He pointed to a replica of Stonehenge. "We believe that in the Pleadon symbolic language the arrangement of these stones spells out: 'Thank you, we had a great time. We'll be back soon.'"

Harris and Roxy looked at each other in amazement.

"I can't believe that so many aliens have visited Earth over the centuries!" Roxy whispered.

Just then, Xad spotted Thaddrix, the Tragonian director of the Museum of Galactic Culture. He was walking toward them.

Xad panicked.

"We can't have him see us with two Earth children!" Xad said to Quar. "How are we going to explain that they snuck onto our ship?"

9 SUPERSTARS!

"I HAVE AN IDEA," SAID QUAR,
reaching into the small backpack she
was carrying. "I brought these along, just
in case we might need them."

Quar pulled out two transformo-
rings. Harris and Roxy had used these
metal rings to disguise themselves as
Tragonians during their visit to Tragas.

"Quickly, place these on your heads," Quar said, handing the rings to Harris and Roxy. "You recall that these transformo-rings project the image of a Tragonian body into the minds of anyone looking at you. This way, no one will know you are from Earth."

Harris and Roxy placed the rings onto their heads. To Zeke, Quar, and Xad—as well as everyone else in the museum—they now looked like they were from Tragas.

Thaddrix hovered over to the group.

"Well, well, if it isn't the stars of the show!" he said. He extended his elbow and touched elbows with Quar and then Xad, the traditional Tragonian greeting.

"Director Thaddrix, it is very nice to see you again," said Quar. "This is our son, Zeke, and his friends."

"Nice to meet you," said Thaddrix. "I must tell you that your exhibit on Earth is the hit of the museum. Why, it's the best thing we've shown in years. So many visitors have said that they were fascinated by your research."

Xad and Quar exchanged glances and smiled, then touched the tips of their tentacles together, a Tragonian sign of affection.

Thaddrix continued. "As a matter of fact, visitors are clamoring for more! They find Earth so fascinating that they want to know everything about it! Why, you two are superstars!"

Quar and Xad looked at each other, shocked. They knew that they did good work, but they had never expected this.

Harris was stunned, too, but in a different way. "Who knew that Earth could be so interesting?" he whispered to Roxy.

"I guess when you live someplace so long, you kind of take it for granted," Roxy replied.

Thaddrix turned to leave. "Well, keep up the good work," he said to Xad and Quar, "wherever your next assignment takes you."

Then he floated off and disappeared from view.

Wherever your next assignment takes you.

These words echoed in Zeke's mind. He had been so caught up in the wonders of the museum, and pride in his parents' work, that he hadn't thought about the fact that their next stop was Earth—and saying goodbye to his friends.

Zeke's mind raced: *Will I ever see Harris and Roxy again?*

Where will I be going next? Another new planet? New culture? New school? New kids? Will I ever be this lucky again in making such good friends?

He sighed as the group headed for the museum's spaceport.

THE SPACESHIP LIFTED OFF from the museum's spaceport and soared toward space. In a few minutes it had left the atmosphere of Kretlak Prime.

"Setting course for the wormhole," said Xad, entering coordinates into the ship's navigation panel. Then he leaned back with a satisfied look on his face. He and Quar smiled at each other, then touched tentacles again.

"We have done well," said Quar.

"Yes, it is very gratifying to hear such nice words from Director Thaddrix," said Xad.

"I find it amazing that he wants more information about Earth!" Quar said.

"Yes," said Xad, scratching his head with two of his tentacles. "In any case, it will be interesting to return to Tragas to receive our next assignment."

"Hmm . . ." said Quar. "'Our next assignment.'"

In another section of the ship, Zeke, Harris, and Roxy sat quietly. They were also all lost in their own thoughts.

Roxy finally spoke. "That museum was great. I was surprised to realize that so many people from all over the galaxy find Earth so interesting. I'm also amazed by what I saw of all the other planets."

Harris turned to Zeke.

"You know, before we met you, we didn't even know that there was life on any planet besides Earth," he said. "Now we've learned not only about you and your family and your planet, but that there is just so much out there that we'll never know."

"And now we're going back to Earth and we'll have to stay there," said Roxy, with a hint of disappointment. "We'll never get to learn about new planets and other species and what they have to offer. Zeke, you are so lucky. You get to move on to the next planet your parents are assigned to and learn all about that world and its people and its culture."

Zeke sighed. "True, but moving around as often as I do makes it very hard to feel like I have a real home. And it's hard holding on to friends—especially good friends like you and Harris."

Just then, Xad's voice boomed throughout the ship.

"Please strap into your seats," he said. "We are about to enter the wormhole."

The three friends each pressed a button on the side of their seats. Several energy straps extended and wrapped around their waists and shoulders. Looking out their viewscreens, they saw the huge spinning, tornado-like entrance to the wormhole. It moved closer and closer.

A few seconds later, the ship entered the wormhole. Everything went dark.

"I can't see anything!" cried Harris.

"That is normal," said Zeke. "A wormhole sucks all light into itself. The darkness will only last a little while."

A few minutes later, the ship emerged out the other side of the wormhole. The space outside the viewscreen was once again filled with stars. Soon, Pluto, Neptune, and Uranus came into view.

"Look!" said Roxy. "We've entered Earth's solar system!"

The rings of Saturn and the giant planet Jupiter came into view next.

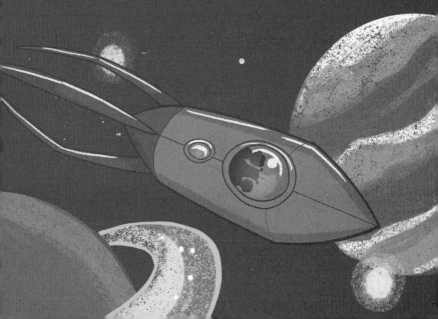

"We're almost home," Harris said sadly. He was glad that he would be seeing his parents soon, but also sad that he'd be saying goodbye to Zeke. "I'm really going to miss you, Zeke."

"Same for me," added Roxy. "I really appreciate the time we got to spend together, getting to know each other."

Mars zipped past the viewscreen, and then Earth finally came into view.

"Wow!" said Roxy. "Earth looks so different from up here. So small. So beautiful! I guess I did always take it for granted."

"Prepare for final descent to Earth," Quar's voice rang out.

"I'll miss you, too," said Zeke. "I don't know where I'm going next, or if I'll ever get to see you two again, but I'm really happy that we're friends!"

Then the ship entered Earth's atmosphere and began to drop down toward the planet's surface, and to Harris's and Roxy's home.

Read on for a sneak peek at the tenth book in the Alien Next Door series!

1

HOME!

A SPACESHIP APPROACHED

Earth, getting ready to land. On board were Zeke and his parents, Xad and Quar, aliens from the planet Tragas. They were returning to their temporary home—Earth. Also on board were Zeke's human best friends, Harris and Roxy, who were on their way back home after an unexpected trip to Tragas.

Xad and Quar were planetary researchers. They had recently completed their research of Earth. Their work was being displayed at the Museum of Galactic Culture on the planet Kretlak Prime. They had just stopped there to view the exhibit on their way back to Earth.

Everyone was on the ship's bridge looking out the front viewscreen. All they could see was a thick bank of clouds as they dropped through Earth's atmosphere.

"Prepare the holo-cloaking display," Quar said, just before they broke through the cloud cover.

"Engaging now," said Xad.

"What's the holo-cloaking display?" Harris asked.

"It hides the ship from anyone on the planet below by projecting another image," Zeke explained. "We use it whenever we land on a new planet so no one knows we have arrived."

"So that's why no one knew that aliens had landed on Earth back when you first came here," said Roxy.

"No one but me!" said Harris.

The three friends laughed. Harris recalled that when Zeke first arrived on Earth, he tried his best to prove that

Zeke was an alien. In time Zeke revealed that Harris's suspicions were correct, and the two became great friends.

"The holo-cloaking display is projecting the image of a thunderstorm to anyone looking up from Earth's surface. All they'll see are thick, dark clouds and flashes of lightning," explained Quar.

Hidden by the projection of a thunderstorm, the ship broke through the cloud layer revealing the ground below to those on board.

"There's my house!" Roxy said excitedly, pointing at the viewscreen.

"And there's mine!" shouted Harris.

"Prepare for final landing," said Quar.

Journey to some magical places, discover monsters, rock out, and find your inner superhero with these other chapter book series from Little Bee Books!

Tales of SASHA
#1
The Big Secret

by Alexa Pearl
illustrated by Paco Sordo

Isle of MISFITS
FIRST CLASS

by JAMIE MAE   illustrated by FREYA HARTAS

ELLA AND OWEN
BOOK 1
THE CAVE OF AAAAAH! DOOM!

by Jaden Kent   illustrated by Iryna Bodnaruk

Mighty MEG
BOOK 1
and the Magical Ring

BY Sammy Griffin   illustrated by Micah Player

A. I. NEWTON always wanted to travel into space, visit another planet, and meet an alien. When that didn't work out, he decided to do the next best thing—write stories about aliens! The Alien Next Door series gives him a chance to imagine what it's like to hang out with an alien. And you can do the same—unless you're lucky enough to live next door to a real-life alien!

ALAN BROWN is an artist who whose work includes the Ben 10: Omniverse graphic novels. He has a keen interest in the comic book world; he loves illustrating bold graphic pieces and strips. He works from an attic studio along with his trusty sidekick, Ollie the miniature schnauzer (miniature in size, giant in personality and appetite), and his two sons, Wilf and Teddy.

LOOK FOR MORE BOOKS IN THE *ALIEN NEXT DOOR* SERIES!